AF269305

NEMIA RISING
EPISODE 0
THE DIG

BY

JOSEPH A. DATTILO

Date Palm Press

All rights reserved. No part of this book may be reproduced, scanned, or distributed in any printed or electronic form without explicit written permission.

All rights reserved. No part of this book may be reproduced, scanned, or distributed in any printed or electronic form without explicit written permission.

First Edition: October 2019

This book is a work of fiction. The names, characters, places and incidents are products of the writer's imagination or have been used fictitiously and are not to be construed as real. Any resemblance to persons, living or dead, actual events, locales, or organizations is entirely coincidental.

Material in this book is for entertainment purposes only. This book is sold with the understanding that neither the author nor the publisher is engaged in rendering technical, legal, space travel, or relationship advice.

Neither the publisher nor the author assume any liability for any errors or omissions or for how this book or its contents are used or interpreted or for any interspecies, interpersonal, or intergalactic consequences resulting directly or indirectly from the use of this book, particularly any use that takes material out of context.

Author: Joseph A. Dattilo

Cover Design: Katherine Dattilo

Distributed by Date Palm Press™, a Date Palm Media LLC division.

Copyright © 2007–2019 by Joseph A. Dattilo

This book is dedicated to my amazing wife, Katherine Dattilo, and my two boys, Vincent and Leonardo, without whom none of my efforts in this or anything else would have any meaning.

To you,

Thank you from the bottom of my heart for supporting my work. I like you. You are clearly an amazing person with impeccable taste in reading material, and I am lucky to be able to count you among my readers.

Right now, you are helping me achieve my dream of bringing the worlds and characters in my mind to life. Right this very moment, we have begun a journey together that I expect to be absolutely glorious, so please turn the page and enjoy the story.

P.S. Don't forget to nag me about the next book (often). Yeah, you thought you were off the hook ... sorry.

Sincerely,
Joe

NEMIA RISING EPISODE 0

THE DIG

HIDING

The boy could feel his blood pulsing against the ring in his sweaty palm as he struggled to run. The desert sand radiated heat beneath his feet, almost nighttime or no, as he flitted across it. He heard the shouts from behind him but dared not look lest he find himself face forward in a pile burning sand.

Why he had grabbed the ring when he saw it? Why hadn't he simply put the ring back when the other workers shouted at him to stop? He did not know. In spite of those questions and his current plight, he pushed forward in the thrall of a rush of adrenaline.

His pursuers were fast, but he was faster. He ducked into the ruins ahead for cover, but there was none to be found. He dashed into an obscured chamber, barely escaping his assailants' sight.

"Come back here, you little rat thief!" came the roar of Mister Nicholson. The burly man's angry voice was all too familiar, but until now, the scrawny boy had managed never to be a target of his wrath. The boy found himself momentarily concerned about the consequences of his actions, but the voices were getting closer, and that left no time for conscience. What was done was done.

He slipped out of the chamber unseen and ran until he came upon an abandoned excavation site and immediately dashed into one of its dark tunnels. What little light there had been outside faded into a faint glimmer behind him. That didn't slow him down—the boy had worked in these tunnels before and, even in the near-dark, could therefore deftly navigate the cracked floors and winding turns almost in silence.

He remembered the pit being covered with tarps when the excavation team left the summer before. As he moved across the covered pit, angry-sounding echoes filled the tunnel, forcing him onto all fours and scrambling to find one of the tarp's edges. His heart raced as caught a corner and slipped quickly beneath it.

Though the floor of the pit was almost painfully uncomfortable, the boy lay as flat as he could, trying to make himself as invisible as he was silent. Clutching the ring with perhaps unnecessary force, he took long, deep breaths to steady his mind. He could hear boots rapping against the hard-stone floor, which nearly unnerved him, but he could no longer hear the men shouting. All he could hear was his own desperately pounding heart, and the thudding of boots as his pursuers searched ever closer.

Now a bright light illuminated the edges of the tarp and its upturned corner—the boy was sure he was caught. Moreover, the light revealed his surroundings, and with a recoil and almost a scream, he could see what had pushed uncomfortably against his face: he was staring into the empty eye sockets of a split-open human skull. He wished he could bring himself to close his eyes, but he wasn't caught yet—and he needed all his senses if he were able, somehow, to get away from the men. Even if that was impossible—but wait.

The varying light shined off something metal inside the skeleton's mouth.

That was important, even if he hadn't formed in his mind in exactly what way. However, he dared not move; the light passed over the tarp several times. But they didn't look under it; he must have done a better job hiding than he thought. After another moment, the sound of the boots on the ground lessened and finally disappeared. That was fortunate, since by this point, black stars were forming from him holding his breath.

He tried to hold off just a little longer to be safe, but his lungs rebelled and forced him to gasp—loudly—for air.

Too loudly.

"Ah, *ha!*" barked a woman's voice. She ripped away the tarp and he was momentarily blinded by artificial light. He moved to stand, but before he rose an inch, the woman's long, smooth fingers brushed against his neck. Then those same fingers grabbed the collar of his shirt and yanked him to his feet. Off his feet, actually.

The boy kicked and screamed at first, but soon gave up, hanging limply in the kind of defeat he hadn't known since ... the last time he had been picked up against his will. Unfortunately, that hadn't been very long before. As he hung there in the woman's weirdly powerful grip, he again went over in his mind all of the bad decisions that had brought him to this point, being hauled out of an abandoned excavation's old pit. He truly had hoped for things to go a little more smoothly.

"Why am I not surprised?" It was his father's voice and rejoiced: *Father was there! He was saved!*

But then ... *Oh, hell. Father was there.* In lieu of an excuse for being there, he shouted at the strong woman, as indignantly as possible, "Lady, I'm gonna give *you* a surprise if you don't let go of me!" But it came out as what it was: a bit of hollow, choked bravado.

In response, the woman tightened her grip, which made his shirt collar squeeze his neck like a noose. She carried him like that out of the tunnel and into the oven-hot air.

"Eoche, let go of my son or you're going to be

another skeleton under that tarp," the boy's father said almost politely, with the kind of calm that belies great menace.

"Of course. And it would do you well to remember that it is *Miss* Eoche, Katsumoto." She stopped and released her hold on the boy's shirt, dumping him face-first into the sand. His father gasped, but if he attempted to stop the fall, none of his muscles had received the signal before it was too late.

This had been exactly what the boy had been running from and trying to avoid—and rightly so, because going face-down into the broiling sand hurt like hell. On the bright side, he could breathe again. Kind of.

"That's *Doctor* Katsumoto."

"Don't forget who pays your bills ... *Katsumoto*," Eoche hissed through clenched teeth, her leather gloves groaning under the strain of her powerfully clenched fists, her deceptively delicate-looking frame absolutely shaking with anger.

"All right, then—why in the hell, *Miss* Eoche, are you dragging Kumogami around the site? What has he done to elicit such a reaction?"

"Why don't you ask the dirty thief himself?" She practically spat the words at the man, but he was concentrated now on examining his son for injury. She took a step of approach but halted when Katsumoto's turned his angry mien towards her.

His expression having hit its mark, he returned his attention to the boy. His voice changed from stern and angry to just stern as he grabbed his son's chin and forced Kumogami's downcast eyes to look into his own. If he was being honest, he was just relieved that it didn't look like his son was any worse for the wear but providing anything but words of discipline in front of his benefactor didn't seem prudent at that moment.

Katsumoto hated that he was always expected to be the disciplinarian. His wife had usually assumed that role, not that he ever could have dragged her out to one of these digs even if they had still been together.

For his part, Kumogami wanted to pry his gaze away from his father's searching eyes but wouldn't have dared try to get away from Father's strong and practiced hold of both chin and eyes even if he could. After some moments of struggle, he sighed and surrendered. A fresh wave of defeat rushed over him as he opened his hand to reveal only to his father the golden coin in his palm.

At Father's unspoken instruction of putting out his own hand, and after what felt like an eternity of silence, Kumogami finally dropped the coin into his calloused palm, this final act of submission cementing to him the reality of his defeat.

Kumogami waited fearfully for his father to speak, but there was not a sound to be heard. Instead, Katsumoto broke eye contact with him and refused to remake it as he slowly stood, pocketing the coin before either Eoche or the until-then–unnoticed team boss, Nicholson, had a chance to see anything. Finally, he snapped his fingers and pointed in the direction of the camp, knowing his message would be immediately clear to his worker.

Nicholson pushed the boy in the direction indicated by Katsumoto, perhaps slightly rougher than was strictly needed and almost flopping him onto his face in the sand again. Eoche started to open her mouth, but Katsumoto motioned for her silence until they were alone.

Eoche, who had been almost growling the entire time, finally unleashed her anger by shouting, "Exactly *what* did that thieving offspring of yours snatch *this* time?"

"This," Katsumoto said, and dropped the coin into the dirt in front of the woman.

"Let me make this clear—"

"No, Eoche, let me make *this* clear," he said icily. "Your gold is not precious enough for me to allow you to put your hands on my son, ever again. Take your trinket—we are done here."

She blinked at him. "Really, Katsumoto?"

"Really," he answered, then turned and headed out of the tunnel.

"The only reason you're even *here* is because of my gold, old man! You *and* your little felon!" she yelled at his back, but he didn't stop or even slow his pace.

Perfect, Eoche thought as she shook her head in disbelief, a single lock of jet-black hair slipping from her normally immaculate coiffure hung mockingly in front of her eyes as she bent and picked up the gold coin.

Another piece of desert crap, she thought. She didn't even bother to toss the coin dramatically over her shoulder; she just dropped it like the piece of desert crap. *Another damned waste of time ... and money.*

THAT NIGHT

That night was the kind of uncomfortable you can feel crawling under your skin. Kumogami lay still and quiet in his cot, trying not to make a sound while he listened to the workers and his father argue outside the tent.

"What were you thinking, bringing him here again?" It was Nicholson that spoke, Kumogami knew that voice, "I understand you've got things going on at home, but come on, Ishi, you know how she reacted last year."

"I know, I know…" was all Katsumoto could muster.

"Besides, what on earth was he thinking!? And all for some stupid coin?" Nicholson sounded more concerned than anything, and there was a long moment of silence between them.

I know, right? Kumogami thought. *What the hell was I thinking?* he had never so much as stolen a pack of gum in his life, he couldn't fathom what had overtaken him. He had been minding his own business and puttering about in the dig site like he usually did at night. Then it caught his eye as he kicked a rock.

"I really can't tell you, Samuel." Katsumoto sounded defeated, and thoroughly drained compared to his usual obnoxiously positive self. "He hasn't acted this way since he was a small child. "Maybe it has to do with his mother leaving. I don't know."

Yeah! Maybe! Wow! Kumogami practically shouted inside, loving his dad's explanation way better than anything he had thought up so far. After all, he was still pretty pissed about her disappearing on them. He tried to hold onto the thought, since it felt a lot better than the alternative theory that he was suffering from early—and sudden—onset kleptomania. Was that even a thing? No, he was pretty sure he would have heard about something *that* interesting from his friends at school. Soon enough, he couldn't hear the conversation outside over his internal disputes, and when it finally did stop, briefly, all he heard was the sound of the campfire outside.

He waited a moment until dismissing the silence and going back to his train of thought. All in all, despite his general level of shame ... for getting caught, mostly ... he was pretty proud of the sleight-of-hand he had pulled off with the ring. He kind of wished he had stuffed the ring in his pocket considering the fact that nobody had even bothered to check them. That said, he was pretty sure his father would have noticed if there *had* been anything in his pockets. His dad had an uncanny eye for small details, which was probably why he was in the business he was. Archeology wasn't exactly the career for someone who lacked attention to detail. Heck, three years prior, it had been Katsumoto who identified the area from flyover footage of an "oddly regular dip in the sand dunes."

Everybody laughed at him back at the university

for all the noise he'd made about that. It had been just another unfunded fantasy that would gather dust on his desk like so many others already had. But, in spite of his colleagues insulting comments, he had still put the grant package together and submitted it for approval. He hadn't expected anything to come of it—after all, nothing had ever come of the dozens of other proposals he had made in the past. The school only funded guaranteed results, and Ishi Katsumoto was bored with the risk-free trips to known sites. He walked away after submitting the papers, feeling a familiar twinge of cold regret mixed with a slight warmth of accomplishment at the same time. He had already begun scouring satellite photos for other areas the next morning when the department head came to tell him the project had been funded by an anonymous donor. There was, of course, a catch, and Katsumoto wasn't sure now if he would have been so eager to move forward with the plan had he known that catch would be the Eoche woman.

Kumogami hadn't really been privy to or interested in the process up to that point, but next thing he knew he found himself in the face-meltingly-hot, mind-numbingly-boring deserts of Arabia. He had always hated the summer but being an albino in 122-degree weather with ten pounds of clothing to keep you from sloughing off skin like a molting half-cooked crayfish took the proverbial cake.

Admittedly, the year prior he had whined and maybe even tried to sabotage a thing or two. That was, at least, until they managed to dig the first twenty feet of tunnel out. After that, he found himself oddly at peace with the whole thing. Said inner peace *may* have had more to do with the twenty-degree temperature drop than anything else, though.

This year, however, had been different. Most of the excavation was focused on the surface of a ruin that had been exposed in a huge sandstorm the previous winter. Kumogami had even looked forward to the time out of school with his father—that was, until the plan was explained to him in detail and he saw the "dig" site for himself.

Kumogami's thoughts raced on as he lay there.

He dreaded the morning sun and wished he could be home for a while longer before his thoughts grew hazy and he slipped into uneasy dreams of beautiful, giant women tossing him back and forth like a helpless, white-haired ragdoll.

MISSING

Much to Kumogami's relief the following morning, one of the camels was gone, together with the ever-oppressive Ms. Eoche. To be perfectly clear, Kumogami didn't have a problem with the camel. If anything, he felt a little bad for it.

The morning was, oddly, otherwise unremarkable. Kumogami even tried to help out a few times, but each time he offered assistance, the crew responded with silent contempt. Apparently, they were still a little ticked-off about that whole "stealing a precious artifact and running away with it" thing. This bothered him less than it usually would have, though, because he spent most of the day—regardless of the task at hand—contemplating how he would retrieve that same precious artifact from the tunnels. He had to figure it out before the dig was over, or—worse—*someone else found it!*

The thought of retrieving it was all-consuming. Luckily, the tunnels weren't really guarded, so he figured that getting to them wouldn't require much more subterfuge than a well-timed slip into the night. That said, actually slipping out was probably going to be more difficult than it would have been before certain recent events had transpired.

He envisioned all sorts of scenarios. There were guards posted at the tunnel entrance, so he could throw a rock or something to get them to leave their posts and investigate. Or, maybe, he could talk his way inside. He shook his head at that one and counted heads at the dig site while he considered the possibilities of someone being gone. But no, everyone was here.

Wait! Everyone was *there!* Right that moment.

Yes!

And not only was everyone busy, but nobody wanted to have anything to do with him even if they weren't. Which, for the first time, felt like a real boon to him. So Kumogami made his way to the tent and waited a few moments to see if anyone showed any interest in his actions. After he was satisfied that nobody cared, he made his way to the other side and exited quietly through the flap. Even with the turban and cloak on, he got hit by the sun like a two-ton anvil in the face. God, how he hated the sun!

He then set out in the direction of the previous year's dig site, shuffling away from the tent slowly but not too slowly, trying not to call attention to himself.

Almost half a mile away, he looked back and found he could just barely make out any details of the camp's tents. The clang of pickaxes had been overshadowed as he escaped, replaced by the shrill sound of sand being picked up and blasted into his face and the surrounding dunes. So, with a little more pep in his step, he trotted on across the hot and unforgiving sandscape, feeling pretty darned good about his clever little self.

Though his eyes, ears, and the inside of his nose all hated him for the sand blown into them, Kumogami managed to get the rest of the way to the tunnels with relatively little problem. By the time he made it there, his heart was pounding with a potent combination of physical exertion and excitement at the fact that he was once again breaking the rules. Well, *kind of* breaking the rules. Or breaking the *kind* of rules. Or whatever—it wasn't like there were any *actual* rules against wandering around in the desert. Or really any rules at all except "Don't get in the way" and "Don't die." His dad really loved to make a big deal about that last one. In any case, more than anything else, Kumogami was excited by the imminent possibility of holding that ring in his hands once again.

Outside the tunnels, he was filled with a familiar awe, as the recently exposed symbol-covered pillars came into view. On the left stood the deeply carved viper with its fangs exposed, ready for the strike. On the right was carved that strangely bird-like serpent. Its now-hollow eye socket stared unnervingly at Kumogami, while its elegant beak pointed skyward. Kumogami found himself once more transfixed before the two pillars, as he had been countless times the summer before, not even noticing the blistering heat or the wind-carried sands around him.

No one on the team the year before had possessed any real expertise in ancient linguistics, and it seemed there was an unusual lack of interest from Mr. Katsumoto in translating the runes, even though Kumogami had expressed his curiosity about them repeatedly. He had always known his father to be curious to a fault, much like himself, but whenever Kumogami attempted to broach the topic of the runes with Father, he had always been quickly ushered into another arduous task that just *needed* to be done. Eventually, not wanting to be instructed to dig another hole or move another rock, Kumogami dropped the subject. But that didn't mean he had to stop wondering, and he stared at the precisely carved rocks, sometimes for hours, tracing the runes over and over with his eyes, as if somehow their meaning would come to him.

***

Suddenly, Kumogami's train of thought was interrupted by the sound of his name being called out from behind him, and as he blinked, he realized the sun had somehow arced halfway across the sky.

How long had he been standing there? It was, as it had been the year before, a gap in time. He didn't know how many times he had stood in that very spot back then, for what often turned out to be hours as he sought meaning in the scratched stone surfaces. Each time before, he had been left a little fuzzy-minded, like when you take a nap for too long in the middle of the day, but it had never been much worse than that.

"Kumogami Narimasu Katsumoto! What on earth are you doing out here again, young man?" It was his father, who seemed angry beyond reason until he saw his son's unexpectedly bewildered face turn toward him.

"Kumo? My God, what happened?" Katsumoto exclaimed as he saw that his son's feet had sunk almost a foot into the blowing sand where he had stood unmoving for god only knew how long. Kumogami's face was a red and bubbling mass wherever it had been exposed to the sun. The white of his cloak and turban contrasted sharply with his broiled face.

Kumogami was confused by his father's transition

from anger to horrified dismay—at least, until he tried to speak. "What's the matt-*heeeeee* ..." he wheezed, the words croaking out oddly, as if they were coming from someone else, and stopped in a horrible gasping choke.

All at once the pain hit him. His knees tried to give way, but his legs were firmly fixed where they had been buried. He instinctively reached up to his face, a decision he instantly regretted as his fingertips sank deep into a large crusty bubble of boiled flesh before they could reach the place his face normally resided. Pain washed up and down his body, covering every inch of him.

He wanted nothing more than to scream, but the energy to do so was not in him. So, instead, he stood there in perfect stillness, his mouth agape in an eerily silent scream.

Katsumoto rushed to his son's side and called out to some workers who had just turned the corner. He had never devoted much thought to the long moments his son had sat in that very spot the year before. Of course, back then, that spot had been covered by an open tent, and the whole crew had been busy excavating the site. For his part, Katsumoto had caught himself staring at the glyphs once or twice, but never in the way his son had been mesmerized. Only now, though, as he held his crumpled boy in his arms, did he realize how different it must have been for his son. His boy's obsession with the mysterious runes was clearly far more than a passing intrigue.

Nicholson frantically dug the boy's feet free from the sand and Katsumoto's tears fell on his son's cracked and blistered skin. He pulled out his canteen and attempted to give some water to the boy. Kumogami choked and sputtered on the few drops that managed to make it to his throat.

As the world moved around him, Katsumoto's mind raced on. Kumogami had always been a quiet and contemplative boy. He would spend long periods pondering in silence, but Mr. Katsumoto had never known his boy to be so entranced by thought as to ignore pain. No, if anything, Kumogami complained of some vague pain on a fairly regular basis. His father couldn't be sure if any of it was real, or if it was just a cry for attention, and the fact that the complaints had only grown worse since his mother left ... well, either she had dealt with the whiny episodes much better than she ever let on, or he was acting out pretty badly. Something which, according to the therapist, was completely normal. That didn't change the fact that it was a complete and total pain in the butt to deal with, though.

Kumogami stared up at his father's eyes, still confused by the waves of pain that rushed over him. The agony surrounded him like a strangely comfortable blanket as it persisted. He could hear his own cries as he was hoisted onto the back of a camel. He saw the sorrow in his father's expression as they journeyed through the desert in the waning daylight. He did not, however, experience these things as he normally would have. The pain was there, he was fairly certain of that, but it was blurred and hazy at the edges. It danced around him as another blurred sense, mixing freely with the strange sights and sounds that all seemed somehow alien to him. He floated across the desert this way for some time. Eventually, though, his own passing thoughts were all that remained. His mind slowly settled as he looked down and imagined the ring on his now deformed and discolored fingers, before thought itself faded into the ever-darkening blur around him.

RECOVERING

Kumogami was yanked into consciousness by men —no soldiers— shouting in a language he couldn't understand. They hurried past him with a blood-soaked man on a gurney. Kumogami opened his eyes little more than a crack, but that made pain rush over his whole face. He slammed them shut again, but too tightly, causing another wave of pain to assault him. He went to put his hands to his face, but stopped short, remembering, faintly, that that had been a bad idea the last time. He wasn't even sure if that memory was real ... regardless, he was willing to err on the side of caution.

He listened as the soldiers shouted orders between one another and heard as what must have been a heart monitor flat-lined in an ominous

continuous beeeeeeeeeeeeeeeeeeeeeeeeeeeee—
. The shouts grew louder, and then there was an ear-
piercingly shrill sound that was cut off by a loud
bang. Then more shouting and then more bangs,
but the sound of the heart monitor never did more
than tremble in its long and ominous whine.

The smell of burnt skin and blood wafted at him,
and he was glad it was too painful to open his eyes.
He wasn't ready to see what he knew must have lay
beside him then. He wondered where he was and
how he had gotten there. Everything was still a blur,
but he remembered going to the tunnels for the
ring. Something had prevented him from getting
there, but what? Everything was hazy past that
point. He had seen the familiar runes, and, next
thing he knew, there had been a blur of pain and
sound that seemed to have lasted ages. He
remembered wisps of color and sound, and the
image of his father's sad eyes. He tried to remember
more, but details eluded him.

He made to sit up, but his whole body felt so
heavy ...

His hands burned as they touched the hard

bedding at his sides. He pushed against it in spite of the pain, but eventually he caved to its forceful demands and sank slowly back into the bedding's Kumogami-shaped dent he had only just stirred from. Despite everything that was going on around him, his mind was consumed with worry about how he would get back to the tunnels—to the ring—in his current condition.

But he wasn't even sure where he was, let alone what had happened to him. Everything was going swimmingly … and then suddenly it was not. Maybe he was still dreaming, yeah maybe he never woke up that night, maybe this is what came after being tossed around by lovely large women. An unpleasant turn of events even by nightmare standards, but it seemed plausible enough to him now that he thought about the alternatives. He was coaxed back into a deep and dreamless sleep by that last comforting thought.

He did not wake again for almost a full day. His body slowly replaced its fluids and struggled to heal the second- and third-degree burns that bubbled over his flesh. His dehydration had been so serious it still threatened to send his body into hypovolemic shock even as it drained through bag after bag of saline.

***

After a few hours of consciousness, Kumogami felt the fog in his mind finally begin to clear. He wished he could just go back to sleep, but he couldn't quietly endure the pain any longer now that it insisted itself to be real. He could just manage to see, through almost-shut eyes, enough to tell that he was in one of those tent-hospitals that dotted the region. Which was totally crazy, considering the nearest *anything* to the camp had been seventy miles away.

To his right, there was a man who, despite being almost fully swathed in white gauze, was attempting to read a book. The gurney on his left, however, lay ominously empty. Kumogami was reminded of the previous night or whenever it had been, and almost shut his eyes again, but just then, he noticed that his father lay snoring on an uncomfortable-looking fold-out chair next to him. A molded-plastic chair with metal legs. the kind usually seen in school cafeterias.

In the current setting, the chair didn't look out of place, but the sleeping man certainly did.

"Father," he managed to choke in a whisper. *"Father."* His voice was a little stronger now. Katsumoto woke with such a start that he fell out of the plastic chair and onto the dirt floor. Katsumoto didn't even bother standing fully—he crawled, as quickly as his shaky limbs could take him, to his boy's side. Tears of joy streamed from his eyes.

"Kumo ..." he said, barely managing to choke out the name through his tears. "You're awake." He sobbed.

Kumogami had been a clumsy kid sometimes, but Katsumoto had never seen so many bandages on anyone, let alone his boy. In fact, before bringing him to the temporary French hospital two nights earlier, the worst thing that had ever happened to Kumogami was the six stitches he got following an apple-cutting incident years earlier. That time, Katsumoto had nearly passed out the moment he saw his son's blood, and his wife had taken over from there.

"Yes, son, what is it?" It had taken a moment to

stop his mind's racing so he could answer Kumogami. He was finally breathing normally again and could feel his heartbeat's fury lessening as he spoke.

"Father, wh ... when can we go beh ... back to the dig?" Kumogami's words were coarse and broken but strangely urgent. They caught Katsumoto completely off guard and there was a long moment of silence between them. Kumogami's nearly translucent eyes were full of excitement as they pled with his father's own puffy eyes. The hunger in his son's piercing gaze was unexpected and sent a shiver up Ishi Katsumoto's spine.

"Kumogami ... we are not going back there. Not now, not ever again."

THE END

That summer had been long, probably the longest of both their lives. Recovery was painful, and neither Kumogami nor his father were ever quite the same after that day. Certainly, they continued to spend time together going through artifacts at the university, but it was nothing like solving puzzles in the field, like what they had done in the past.

Katsumoto had tried to protect his son from all he could from then on, but, as the boy grew older and the work more demanding, it was only natural that they began to grow apart. Inevitably came the day when Kumogami stood alone. His eyes locked on his father's still form, knowing what to do but not wanting to do it. Perhaps he thought delaying his part would somehow put things right again.

He tried to avert his eyes, but they lingered on

the kimono where it crossed, right over left. It was then, as white wisps of cold fog rose from around the man's still and serene sides, that Kumogami finally accepted the truth of his loss.

His father had been ill for at least a year, though it never stopped him from continuing his work. The dig in Arabia may have been his last archaeological trip outside the country, but that didn't mean he couldn't continue to pursue his interests. Katsumoto was never able to get over the remorse that plagued him for the injuries his son had sustained that day. Kumogami, of course, had enjoyed the extra attention at the time, but now he felt guilt's knife twisting in his back as he considered whether his father's faltering morale and health had been *his* doing.

Kumogami lovingly doused his father's lips with water and dropped his lucky hardwood excavation tool beside him. The tool fell with a hollow sound among the many unfamiliar burnable trinkets that his father's coworkers and students had left at the man's side. Just another reminder that, this time tomorrow, his father would be no more. Perhaps his spirit would make its way to another plane, or perhaps what burned tomorrow was truly all that was left of the man, the man who had nurtured and taught him almost everything he knew, or at least all that was truly worth knowing. Kumogami was the only family Katsumoto had at the end. Both his grandparents had long since passed, and, since leaving them, his mother had never once made any effort to contact them. That said, the wake was filled to the brim with the many people who his father had touched in life. The growing pile of black and silver envelopes with condolence money gave Kumogami a rough idea of how many were in attendance, but he tried not to look at them as he took his seat in the front row.

He rolled the prayer beads in his hands; they felt cold against his skin. It felt weird holding them—and being in the temple in general. Kumogami wasn't exactly big on rituals or traditions. At least, he wasn't big on the kinds of rituals and traditions that other people seemed to care about. He was a little more than borderline OCD … oh, who was he kidding, he was full-blown OCD, so he was plenty familiar with his own slate of rituals. Of course, his rituals were important, unlike all the silly ones that other people seemed to care so much for.

The Buddhist priest walked silently to the front of the room and began to chant a deep and rhythmic sutra that flowed in waves over the floor and up Kumogami's feet and ankles. It felt like his body was being engulfed in honey or molasses. It was thick and sweet, and it filled him with an unexpected calmness.

It had probably been years since Kumogami had last thought of his time at the dig site with his father, but for some reason it all rushed to his mind while the sutra washed over him. Life has a way of blurring what is important, and death has a way of revealing it, always far too late. Despite the unpleasant way the trip had ended, that time had been one of Kumogami's greatest adventures and one of the last times he remembered seeing his father smile in his once familiar and jovial way. In truth, the experience had forced the both of them to grow up—more, perhaps, than it should have.

Then, as quickly as clarity and comfort had set in,

it ended as the sutra suddenly ceased. Silence filled the room and crept back into Kumogami's mind. The long strands of silver hair that flowed over his back were all that moved around him, as, one by one, each of the mourners passed silently into the night. This all passed as a blur until at last there was only one other mourner left. Kumogami hadn't seen the big, burly man in at least half a decade, but there he stood, lingering over his father's ever still form. It was Nicholson.

Time did not move at a normal pace then, instead lingering around the edges of things much like that blurry time long past. The flickering flames of the many candles seemed to creep from brightness to dark like a slow wave creeps onto the beach only to wash back out to sea. The boy in the black kimono felt a different world around him then, and, however brief that moment of clarity, it changed him. He saw Nicholson's tear-stricken and clean-shaven face approach him, but Kumogami made no move to acknowledge the man. He wanted to thank him, to wrap his arms around him as he had as a child, but his eyes and mind remained still fixed on where his father lay.

Kumogami felt Nicholson's firm and comforting grip on his shoulder. He heard the man choke out, "I'm sorry." Then Nicholson's footsteps faded, and it was once again as it had been before, even if just this last time. It was just him and his father, alone together again. So, the sleepless nights' vigil carried on. He had dreaded this part before, but now that it had begun, it didn't seem so bad. College and his work had consumed most of his faculties of late, and the dark quiet that surrounded him now was oddly comforting and distantly familiar.

Life in Tokyo was loud, in spite of its best efforts to be a respectful and quiet place as is the Japanese tradition. The reality of cramming millions of people into one small area didn't lend much to the dream and wish of quiet, though. Tokyo had personality and a rich history, but it was full of other things, too ... teenagers, for one, and lots of them. Following the difficult footsteps of his father in school had been anything but calming of late, particularly considering the fact that he had to endure the *pleasure* of sitting alongside many of those same teenagers he cared so little for. He felt this way in spite of the fact that he was technically a teenager, himself. He often consoled himself by saying it was only a technicality.

Everyone called Kumogami an old soul, and that was cool with him so long as it meant he could continue to get his work done in silence. It struck the young man then how much, as a young child, he had ridiculed his father for his choice of profession, how much he had complained that his father worked too much, and how he now found himself working the same hours and chasing the same dreams his father had. He even ended up going to school to enter his father's field, archeology. Kumogami, unlike his father, specialized in linguistics. All of human history was just a puzzle to him, a web of secrets best unraveled through words contained in the ancient texts that survived into the modern world. Eventually everything might be neatly explained and just as neatly categorized in front of him. That was the idea, at least, but it never seemed to turn out that cleanly in practice. He hoped that, in time, that much would improve.

He mused on these and many other things in silence through the night. With the rise of the sun came those who would partake in the funerary proceedings that day. Nothing of particular note occurred: the faces were the same, or maybe different; he didn't know or care. Lack of sleep and a lack of familiarity with his father's friends or even acquaintances made the proceedings little more than a sea of sullen faces and a ripple of black kimonos not so different from his own.

He joined some of those unfamiliar faces in carrying the wooden casket, but in the end, it was he, and he alone, who watched as the casket made its slow journey through the flame and into the air. It was only he who watched the last wisps of smoke rise up into air from what once had been his father, and it was only he who stumbled out afterward into the darkness of night, completely and utterly alone.

INHERITANCE

He was glad for the numbness that had set in during the day. He cared little for whether it was from lack of sleep or something worse he would otherwise be concerned about, so long as it remained. As long as he could continue to put one foot in front of the other, everything would be okay. Or, at least as okay as it was likely ever to be again.

The journey on the bullet train was longer than usual, or at least it felt that way. The trip was never actually longer from one day to another, another point of pride for the city and its very efficient denizens.

By halfway through the trip, things were starting to blur. At some point as he rode in silence, pressed shoulder-to-shoulder with his fellow passengers, he realized he was crying. Until that moment, none of it had quite felt real, but then and there the loss hit him, and hit him hard. So hard that it threatened to take his feet out from beneath him. Of course, the train was packed so tight that he doubted he could have fallen to the floor if he had tried. For the first time in his life, he was a little bit glad to be packed into the cab with the other sardines. The other passengers more or less politely ignored him while involuntarily providing his wavering frame the small gift of support it needed to stay upright. They passed street after street, the tears that streamed silently down his cheeks showing no sign of stopping.

The tears finally dried as they passed the Inokashira Koen park. He pulled out his handkerchief and wiped his nose as discreetly as he could. The light from various cafe and bar signs glared uncomfortably into his tear-blurred eyes, making it hard for him to keep them open. Each time the train stopped; it was like a strange wave of people flowing around him. He stood stock still, never moving an inch as they filed out in unison, each replaced by another person who always looked just as ordinary as the one who had just left. It felt to

Kumogami like the sea of people around him was an organism unto itself, each individual unknowingly playing his or her part in making up the great beast they called a city. He usually didn't give this experience much thought, but, as empty as he was inside then, he felt almost as though he were watching it all happen from outside himself. It was strange and surreal, and he very nearly missed his stop at the Kichijoji Station. He had grown so used to the stops not being of consequence to him that he hadn't noticed it until the train's familiar computerized voice jarred him from his trance.

He shook his head, trying to fight the haze, and almost waited too long before allowing himself to be carried out the door by the current of outgoing passengers. He only just managed to slip through a crack in the crowd before he would have been carried right back where to he had just been. Feeling instinctively for his keys, he carried on, trying to focus on their familiar feel in his fingers. Normally it was a relief to see the post office or his favorite restaurant, but tonight he was filled with foreboding as he passed them.

The Kichijoji district hadn't decided to sleep just yet. The sidewalks, and businesses were busy as they always seemed to be. It was both entertaining and annoying to see the long lines that formed outside businesses even as night closed in. Entertaining because the other businesses that, in Kumogami's estimation, were just as good or even better stood all but empty beside the other place's long queues; but annoying because he always had to navigate his way around the waiting people on his way home from work or school. Not to mention, they were always so loud he could hear them even from inside his house.

Coming back there after the serene silence of the night before in the remote temple was painful in many ways. The noise and light that attacked his senses was one thing but knowing without a doubt he was the only one who would be home when he got there ... *that* was another thing altogether. It wasn't like Kumogami and his father talked much or even spent much time together anymore, but that wasn't the point. Before that night, they might have had a conversation, they might have watched the local news together, or maybe seen each other in the hallway. There had always been the comfort of each other's presence even when they didn't really have anything to say or do together. Now that comfort was gone forever. Whether his father was to be reborn as a giraffe, waiting for him on some higher plane of existence, or simply no more ... the fact was that he was gone, and he wasn't coming back.

It took him longer than usual, though it wasn't far, but eventually he reached the gate to their—*his* alone, now, he guessed—home. He shuddered at the word 'his' as it taunted him by replacing the familiar 'our' of just days before. The house was a nice, modern home. It was built on land that had been in the family for generations. Kumogami might have even liked it there if it wasn't for where it was. He probably would have liked it a lot more when his family originally acquired it, but that had been a long time ago when things in Tokyo moved much more slowly. Now, of course, it was only a block away from the most popular shops and pubs in the district, nothing like what he wished it was.

The paper-covered family shrine caught his eyes as he walked, filling him with a deep sadness and making the three steps to his front door the longest he had ever taken. Eventually, he managed to pull his keys from his pocket. He tried to push them into the lock, but to his surprise, the large wooden door swung slowly inward with a low, ominous creak. A shiver ran up his spine; he hadn't even put the key halfway in.

What the hell? Kumogami's eyes opened wide, and he woke instantly from his former daze. *I closed the door, right? I always close the door!* Kumogami felt a rush of adrenaline as thoughts of a terrible intruder raced through his mind. Were they still here? What could they have taken?' However, as he peered fearfully inside, nothing looked amiss. The house seemed as immaculate as ever.

He sighed with relief. Even though he had been occupied by going to his father's funerary proceedings, he had his doubts that he had somehow forgotten to close the door. But, seeing nothing else amiss and wanting nothing more than to sleep until this whole nightmare could be properly compartmentalized in a dark corner of his mind, he pressed forward. He argued with his inner voice, ignoring it as it implored him to turn around and run.

He took his shoes off and absent-mindedly put his black kimono on a hanger in the closet. He walked slowly down the hall, peering with instinctive fear down the dark corridor to the kitchen. He flipped the lights on in spite of how comfortable it was to be wrapped in kind darkness. He couldn't help but avert his eyes and close them tightly as the bright lights flickered to life. Squinting, he looked around, but nothing unusual caught his eyes. The bowl of fruit was still in the middle of the table, the toaster and rice maker exactly where they belonged. Everything was as immaculate as ever.

He flipped the light switch back off and shook his head. *You freaking left the house unlocked ... idiot.* He continued to chastise himself as he made his way up the steep stairs to the bathroom and set about brushing his teeth.

He did not hear the sound of his bedroom door opening slowly behind him, nor did he see the shadow pass silently through the hallway only inches behind him. He carried on in his usual routine and prepared himself for the sleep he craved so much.

He made his way toward the bedroom, consciousness drifting away as he moved closer to his bed. His mind gleefully encouraged him to prepare for the sleep, and his limbs grew heavier the closer he got. He pulled his covers back lazily and began his slow ascent to his comfortable pillow's embrace.

He felt the cool sharp edge on his fingertips as they brushed against the pillow, and thought, *that sure is cold*. He was about to rest his head on it when his fading consciousness was ripped back into full throttle.

Wait a second—cold and sharp.

He jumped in the air like a cat who had just caught sight of an unexpected cucumber. Frantically, he flipped the lights on and stared fearfully at his bed. His heart raced and his chest heaved as the blood whooshed back into his head and extremities. There, upon his pillow, was a small hand-written note and an intricately carved black box.

He remained still for some time, pressed hard against the wall, not knowing what to do. He walked forward tentatively and reached down slowly, his fingers trembling from his fear as they wrapped around the note.

> I am truly sorry for your loss, child. Your father made me promise to deliver this to you in the event of his death, and though I had hoped it wouldn't have come before my own … but that is not how things worked out.
>
> I wanted to give it to you personally, to see you again, but Ishi's instructions were clear, and I promised.
>
> With love, as always,
> A friend

He read the words several times. *A friend?* What, a friend who had broken into his home and put this there? Why couldn't they have just given whatever it was to him personally? And, most importantly, what was with the box? These and many other questions rushed through his mind as he pored over the note over and over again. He read and re-read each word until the letters on the page began to look like a jumble of foreign symbols with no meaning at all.

He dropped the letter, allowing it to flutter back down upon his pillow as he pulled his phone out. His mind raced as his fingers hovered over the icon for emergency services, but as much as he wanted to, he could not bring himself to press it.

Instead, overcome with curiosity, he set the phone down and picked up the small, black-stained wooden box. It was heavier than he expected, and he almost dropped it as he tried to delicately lift it from his bed. The reason for its heaviness became clear as soon as he flipped it open. Though the box was wood on the outside, the inside was cast from thick metal, probably lead, judging from the weight and color. He found himself most interested in the fact that the box was lead-lined. *What could possibly need to be in a lead ...*

His thoughts never finished, interrupted as the contents of the box were finally revealed.

The familiar glint of gold and an almost-living amber met his eyes again for the first time in many years. Immediately, he was filled with a distantly familiar lustful zeal as he looked at what *had* to be the ring from many years before. He picked it up eagerly, bathing in the rush of energy that washed over him as it touched his skin. How long had his father had it? Who had left it for him? He ultimately concluded he didn't really care anymore. His mind buzzed as he placed the ring gingerly onto his right index finger. It felt good. It felt right. It felt like it had always belonged there, like it had just been missing all along.

At the bottom of the box was a small and slightly yellowed piece of paper. He immediately recognized his father's handwriting and the Kanji symbol that Ishi Katsumoto had, with obvious great care, inscribed upon the paper's surface.

Be strong, be brave.

Thank You,

Thank you so much for joining me! I hope you enjoyed reading this story as much as I enjoyed creating it. If you liked this book, then you will love *Nemia Rising: Twin Dragons Wake*. Having written *Twin Dragons Wake* first, I think this prequel brings even more life to Kumogami and the world in which he and many others have long lived in my mind.

Be sure to join my email list from NemiaRising.com to be the first to know when the next book in the series has been released and to get early discounted pricing on anything else, I write in the future. If you enjoyed this book and have the time to share your experience with other readers in the form of a review, it would go a long way toward making it possible for me to continue to dedicate the long hours it takes to create these worlds for you.

When you are ready to dive deeper and experience more of Kumogami's adventures, *Twin Dragons Wake* already awaits you. Watch as the hinges of his world are rocked even further, and the lines between illusion and reality blur beyond distinction. The world of *Nemia Rising* is full of mysteries that even I, its creator, have yet to unlock. But, as we journey together, you and I, its secrets will reveal themselves to us.

Again, the link to join and learn more about the series is NemiaRising.com. I look forward to hearing about your impressions of this book and seeing you online or even in person!

Sincerely,
Joseph Dattilo

www.ingramcontent.com/pod-product-compliance
Lightning Source LLC
Chambersburg PA
CBHW021344060726
47591CB00006B/2159